# Wee Granny's

That's her

# BAG

What's in there?

Picture Kelpies

To Rachel, Andrew and Hannah with love

Picture Kelpies is an imprint of Floris Books
First published in 2011 by Floris Books

www.florisbooks.co.uk
The publisher acknowledges subsidy from Creative Scotland towards the publication of this volume.
British Library CIP Data available
ISBN 978-086315-844-5
Printed in China

Emily and Harry were excited. They were waiting for Wee Granny to arrive. She was taking them to the park while Mum helped get ready for the school fair.

They loved going places with Wee Granny. They hoped she'd bring her tartan bag. Surprising things always happened when Wee Granny brought her bag.

Last Christmas Wee Granny and the children went carol singing.

When Harry's candle burned right down to a stump, Wee Granny reached into her tartan bag and pulled out...

...a lamp-post to help him see!

Last summer Wee Granny took the children to the seaside. When they got to the beach she reached into her tartan bag and pulled out…

...three deckchairs! Stripy ones for herself and Harry, and a pink one for Emily, because that was her favourite colour.

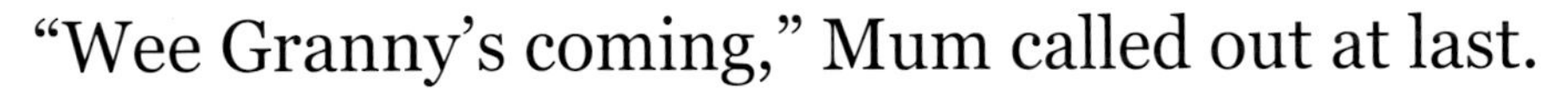

“Wee Granny’s coming,” Mum called out at last.

“Hello, my bonnie darlings,” Wee Granny said. “I’ve brought sandwiches and orange juice for our picnic in the park.”

“Thank you, Wee Granny,” said Emily and Harry.

“Have a nice time,” Mum said as she waved them goodbye. “And remember to be good.”

“Would you like to sit down, Wee Granny?” Emily asked when they reached the park. “On a deckchair, perhaps?”

“Let’s find a picnic bench,” replied Wee Granny.

While Wee Granny was getting the picnic things from her bag, the children tried to peek inside, but she snapped it shut.

Harry couldn’t stand it any longer. “Wee Granny,” he asked, “did you bring anything else in your bag?”

“I’ve brought my phone,” Wee Granny said. “You never know when someone might call.” Emily and Harry were disappointed.

Then they heard a ringing noise coming from Wee Granny's bag.
She reached inside and pulled out...

TELEPHONE
TELEPHONE

…a bright red, old-fashioned telephone box!

“I won’t be long, my bonnie darlings,” she said, stepping inside the box and closing the door.

The children stared, wide-eyed, as they watched Wee Granny chattering inside.

“That was your mum,” Wee Granny said, coming back out. “They need more cupcakes for the school fair. She’s asked me to make some. Will you help, my bonnie darlings?”

“Yes please!” yelled the children. They loved baking.

“I’ll need a big mixing bowl,” said Wee Granny.
“I’m sure I’ve got one in here somewhere.”
She rummaged in her tartan bag
and brought out a bowl.

“And I need kitchen scales, a
cupcake tin,
flour,
butter,
sugar
and eggs.”

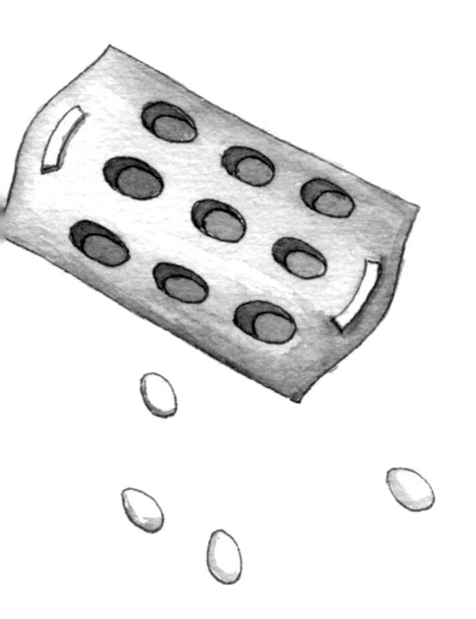

“And of course, to bake the cakes, I’ll need a nice hot oven,” Wee Granny said, peering inside her bag.

Harry and Emily looked at each other and shook their heads. No one, not even Wee Granny, could carry an oven around in her bag. Could she?

“Be careful, my bonnie darlings,” Wee Granny said, placing the oven on the ground. “Don’t go too close. It’s very hot.”

Everyone was busy weighing and measuring and mixing. Soon a warm smell of baking filled the park.

"Time to do the washing-up," Wee Granny said when the children had scraped the baking bowl clean.

Wee Granny reached into her tartan bag...

“Oh, deary me,” she sighed. “I forgot to bring the kitchen sink. We’ll have to wash the dishes in the pond. Quick, my bonnie darlings. People are starting to stare.”

Emily and Harry looked up to see a small crowd gathering around them.

By the time they'd finished washing up, the cupcakes were ready. They placed them carefully inside some boxes – you can probably guess where they got the boxes.

"Uh, oh," said Harry, "I can see a policeman."

"Hurry, children," said Wee Granny, "let's clear everything away."

Wee Granny opened up her bag and in went...

Police

...the eggs, the sugar,
the butter, the flour,
the cake tin,
the kitchen scales
and the mixing bowl.

“Wow,” whispered Harry and Emily as they watched Wee Granny *squeeeeeze* the enormous oven into her tartan bag.

Then Wee Granny closed her bag, put it under her arm and took the children to the school to meet their mum and Mrs Graham, their teacher.

BOOKS
Cake
£1

“Thank you, Wee Granny,” said Mrs Graham. “Now we’ve got lots of cakes to sell on Saturday.” And she gave the children a cupcake each for helping.

“Don’t eat them until you’ve had your supper,” said Mum.

“Can we put them in your bag, Wee Granny?” asked Harry.

“Of course,” said Wee Granny. “I don’t have much in it today.”

“But what about...?”

“Shhh now, Emily,” said Wee Granny. “It’s time to go home.”

The SWEET Sh

“Are you coming to the school fair on Saturday?” asked Emily on the way home.

“Of course, my bonnie darling,” said Wee Granny. “I’m going with Bert.”

“Who’s Bert?” asked Harry.

“Bert’s my friend,” said Wee Granny. “Would you like to meet him?” The children nodded.

Wee Granny reached into her tartan bag and pulled out…

"Bert and I are in charge of the donkey rides," said Wee Granny.

"Wow!" said Emily.

"Wee Granny?" said Harry. "Is your bag magic?"

"Of course not," said Wee Granny with a wink. "I just like to be prepared."

he SWEET Shop